「だいじょうぶ。時計の針はかならず重なるから」

"Don't worry. The two hands will surely meet."

町のはずれにあるホタルの森のなかに、
こわれていないのに11時59分で針が止まっている
ふしぎな時計台がありました。
そこに住むヘンクツジジイのチックタックは、それでもまいにち、
歯ぐるまの手入れをしています。
「この時計は、こわれてなんかおらん」
「こわれてないのに動かないなんて、おかしいじゃないですか」
修理にきた役場の男は、歯ぐるまにさわらせてもらえません。
あの日から止まったまんま。きょうも12時の鐘は鳴りません。

In the middle of a wood full of fireflies, on the edge of the town, stood a strange clock tower. It wasn't broken, and yet the two hands had stopped at 11:59. In it lived crotchety old Mr. Tick-Tock.
But though he was a crotchety old man,
he took good care of the clock's cogwheels every day.
"This clock's not broken!"
he declared when the town hall repairman came to fix it.
"Well, it's strange that it doesn't work, even though it's not broken."
But Mr. Tick-Tock wouldn't let the repairman touch the cogwheels.
There the clock sat, with its hands forever stuck at 11:59.
They hadn't moved since that day years ago.
Another day, and once again there was no sound from the chimes
that should ring at 12 o'clock.

時計の針がひるの12時をさし、鐘の音がひびきました。
「よるの12時にきく鐘は、もっと感動するぜ」
住みこみではたらくチックタックは、
この時計台のことならなんでもしっています。

Ding-dong!
The two hands of the clock pointed to 12 o'clock,
and the chimes rang out.
"It's even more amazing when you hear them strike midnight!"
Mr. Tick-Tock lived in the clock tower in order to look after the clock,
and he knew everything about it.

「ねえ、チックタック、きのう、
孤児院(こじいん)にあたらしいなかまがやってきたよ。
まえにいた町(まち)が、火(ひ)の鳥(とり)におそわれたんだって」
『火(ひ)の鳥(とり)』というのは、火(ひ)の雨(あめ)をふらすおそろしい雲(くも)で、
ここさいきん、いろんなばしょで発生(はっせい)しているようです。

"Somebody new turned up at the orphanage yesterday, Tick-Tock.
Apparently the town where she was living was attacked
by the Fire Bird."
The Fire Bird was a scary cloud that poured down a rain of fire.
It had appeared in a lot of places recently.

彼女の名前はニーナ。すっかり町の人気もの。
「ニーナちゃん。このスイカをもってきな」
「ありがとう、おじさん。あまったら、
カブトムシにもわけてあげる」
ニーナは、孤児院ではカブトムシの飼育係をまかされています。

Her name was Nina. Everyone in the town loved her.
"Here you are, Nina, have some watermelon."
"Thank you! If there's any left over,
I'll share it with the rhinoceros beetle."
Nina was the one who looked after the pet rhinoceros beetle
in the orphanage.

つぎの日。ニーナが時計台にあそびにきました。
「時計台のなかに入ったの、はじめて」
「おい！　はしりまわるな！　時計は精密機械だぞ」
チックタックが注意をしても、
ニーナはまるできこうとしません。
いわんこっちゃない。
ニーナは、ぬけた床に足をとられて、スッテンコロリン。
そのひょうしに、歯ぐるまをこわしてしまいました。

The next day, Nina came to visit Mr. Tick-Tock in the clock tower.
"This is my first time to go inside a clock tower!"
"Hey! Stop that running around!
Clocks are delicate instruments, you know!"
But though Mr. Tick-Tock warned her,
Nina didn't bother listening. Silly girl!
Oops! Suddenly, she tripped on a loose floorboard
and down she tumbled.
When she fell, she broke a precious cogwheel.

「ごめんなさい！」
「だからいっただろ」
チックタックはニーナをひっぱって、
町(まち)の部品屋(ぶひんや)にはしります。

"I'm so sorry!"
"I told you, didn't I?"
Mr. Tick-Tock grabbed Nina and pulled her along
to the town hardware shop.

「この歯ぐるまと、このネジをください」
チックタックが買いものをするとなりで、
ニーナが小さくなっています。

"I want one of these cogwheels and these screws please."
Nina stood there beside him feeling very small
while he made the order.

「どう？　なおりそう？」
「だいじょうぶ。ずっと、コイツとつきあってきたんだ」
油まみれのチックタック。時計の修理はお手のもの。
ゴロゴロゴロゴロ歯ぐるまが、たちまち動きだしました。

"Is it okay? Do you think you can fix it?"
"No problem. I know this clock like the back of my hand."
Mr. Tick-Tock was covered in oil.
Repairing the clock was his specialty.
And in no time, the cogwheels rumbled into action again.

「ねえ、ニーナ、しってる？
ながい針はだいたい1時間にいちどは、
みじかい針に追いつくんだけど、
11時台だけは追いつかないんだよ」
チックタックが話すと、時計にも人のこころがあるかのようです。
「ふたつの針がつぎにかさなるのは、12時。
そこで、やっと会えるんだ」
「なんだか、恋人どうしみたいね」

"Hey, Nina, did you know this?
Once every hour, the big hand moves past the little hand of the clock.
But only between 11 and 12, that doesn't happen."
To hear Mr. Tick-Tock talk, you'd think clocks have hearts,
just like we do.
"The next time the two hands come together will be at 12 o'clock.
That's when they finally meet."
"They're just like lovers, aren't they?"

「ごめんチックタック。待った!?」
「ニーナはいつも待ちあわせ時間ギリギリにくるなぁ」
「アウト?」
チックタックはくびを横にふり、笑顔でいいました。
「ギリギリセーフ!」

"Sorry, Mr. Tick-Tock! Did I keep you waiting?"
"You always come just in the nick of time, don't you, Nina?"
"So, I'm late?"
Mr. Tick-Tock shook his head and smiled.
"No, you just made it."

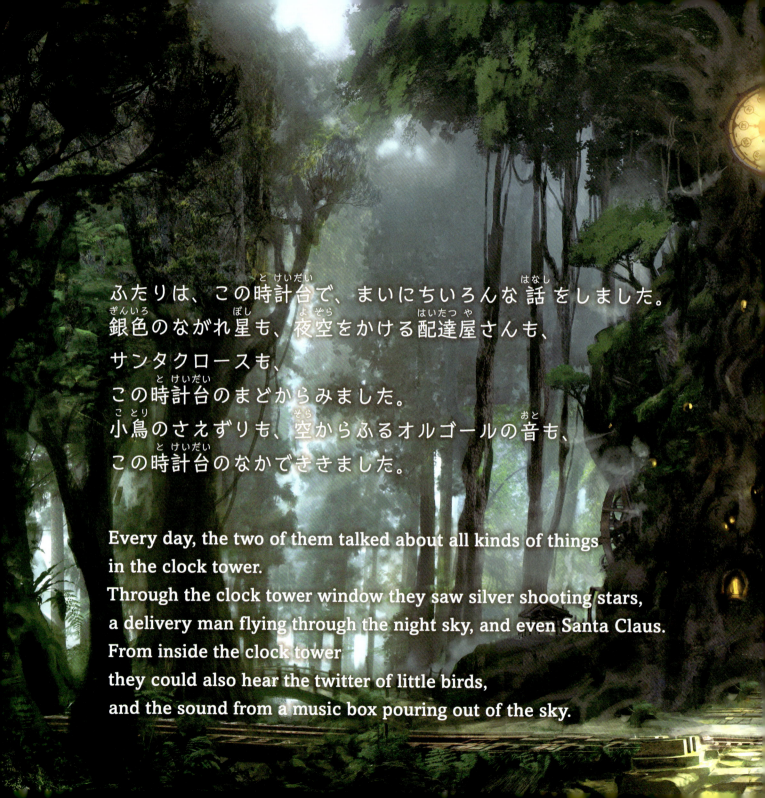

ふたりは、この時計台（とけいだい）で、まいにちいろんな話（はなし）をしました。
銀色（ぎんいろ）のながれ星（ぼし）も、夜空（よぞら）をかける配達屋（はいたつや）さんも、
サンタクロースも、
この時計台（とけいだい）のまどからみました。
小鳥（ことり）のさえずりも、空（そら）からふるオルゴールの音（おと）も、
この時計台（とけいだい）のなかできこえました。

Every day, the two of them talked about all kinds of things
in the clock tower.
Through the clock tower window they saw silver shooting stars,
a delivery man flying through the night sky, and even Santa Claus.
From inside the clock tower
they could also hear the twitter of little birds,
and the sound from a music box pouring out of the sky.

ある日、ニーナがいいました。
「あのね、チックタック。わたし、
あなたにいえなかったことがあるの」
「だいじょうぶ。ぜんぶ、うけとめるよ」
チックタックは耳をピョンッと立てました。
「ごめん。ありがとう」
ニーナはそういうと、ワンピースのそでをまくります。

One day, Nina said to Mr. Tick-Tock,
"You know, there's something I've never been able to tell you."
Mr. Tick-Tock pricked up his ears.
"Don't worry, whatever it is, I'm happy to hear it."
"Thank you. Okay, here goes."
With these words, Nina rolled up her sleeve.

「なんだい、それは？」
「ヤクの木よ」
呪われた島『太鼓島』にしか生えていないヤクの木が、
ニーナのうでに生えています。
「ほうっておくとドンドン大きくなるの」

"Oh my, what's that?"
"It's a Flame Tree."
 Sure enough, a Flame Tree, a tree which only grew on enchanted
 Drum Island, was growing on Nina's arm.
"But if you don't do something, it will grow bigger and bigger."

「わたしのおかあさんも、おなじ呪(のろ)いにかかっていたの」
「おかあさんは？」
「からだから生(は)えてきた木(き)にのまれて、木(き)になった」

"The same magic spell was cast on my mother."
"What happened to her?"
"She was swallowed by the tree that grew out of her body,
 and she became a tree."

「キミもおかあさんみたいに
木になってしまうんじゃないかと、心配なんだね？」
チックタックが話しはじめました。
「植木職人のトムじいさんに相談すれば、
木の生長を遅らせることができる。
ニーナ、だいじょうぶだよ」

"And you're worried that you'll become a tree
 just like your mother did, right?"
Then Mr. Tick-Tock went on.
"If we talk to old Tom the Gardener,
 he can make the tree grow more slowly.
 Don't worry, Nina!"

すっかり日が暮れたので、チックタックはニーナを孤児院まで
おくることにしました。
「ねえ、ニーナ。よるの12時の鐘を、
時計台できいたことはないだろ？」
「あたりまえじゃない。孤児院には門限があるんだから」
「よるはね、鐘の音で目をさましたホタルたちが、
いっせいにかがやきだすんだ。
まるで星空のなかにいるようなんだよ」
「きいてみたい。よる12時の鐘を、時計台のなかで、
ふたりできいてみたい」

Night had already fallen, so Mr. Tick-Tock decided to
take Nina back to the orphanage for the night.
"Hey, Nina. I don't think you've ever heard the clock chime
midnight at the clock tower, have you?"
"Of course not. I have to get back to the orphanage
before the curfew time, you know."
"When the clock chimes at night, the fireflies all wake up and
begin to shine. It's just like being in the middle of a starry sky."
"Oh, I want to hear it! I want to be in the clock tower with you
to hear the clock strike midnight!"

「来月、院長先生がるすにするから、
そのよるなら孤児院をぬけだせる！」
「きまりだね。よるの12時の鐘をふたりできこう！　約束だよ！」
「うん。約束」
しかし、その約束がはたされることはありませんでした。

"One night next month the head of the orphanage will be away,
so I can sneak out and join you!"
"Right, it's a deal. Let's listen to the midnight chimes together!
It's a promise!"
"Yes, it's a promise."
But that promise was not fulfilled.

三日後、悲劇はとつぜんやってきました。
町に警報がひびきわたり、まもなく、大きな大きな黒い雲が
空をおおいました。火の鳥です。
火の鳥は火の雨をふらせ、
町はいっしゅんにして炎につつまれました。
孤児院からともだちがかけこんできました。
「ぶじだったか？　町のみんなは！？」
「みんなは地下に逃げこんだ。でも……」

Suddenly three days later, tragedy struck.
Alarm bells sounded in the town, and in no time a huge black cloud had covered the sky. It was the Fire Bird!
The Fire Bird rained down fire everywhere,
and in an instant the town was enveloped in flames.
Nina's friends at the orphanage came running to the clock tower.
"You're okay? How about everyone in the town?"
"Everyone escaped underground, but…"

「ニーナがみつからないんだよ！」

"We can't find Nina!"

チックタックは時計台をとびだし、町に向かいました。
あたまのなかに、あの日の会話がよみがえります。
「きいてみたい。よる12時の鐘を、時計台のなかで、
ふたりできいてみたい」
「きまりだね。よるの12時の鐘をふたりできこう！　約束だよ！」
「うん。約束」

Mr. Tick-Tock rushed out of the clock tower and ran to the town.
In his head he could hear the conversation they had that day.
"Oh, I want to hear it! I want to be in the clock tower with you
to hear the clock strike midnight!"
"Right, it's a deal. Let's listen to the midnight chimes together!
It's a promise!"
"Yes, it's a promise."

「ニーナ！　ニーナ！」
チックタックの声は、炎の音に、かきけされてしまいます。
町の人たちも、火をかわし、がれきをかきわけ、
けんめいにニーナをさがします。
ニーナは町じゅうの人から愛されていました。
そしてだれよりも、チックタックから。

"Nina! Nina!"
But though Mr. Tick-Tock kept calling her name,
his voice was lost in the roar of the flames.
The townsfolk were desperately searching for Nina, too,
running hither and yon among the flames and pushing
through the rubble.
Everyone in the town loved Nina.
And Mr. Tick-Tock loved her more than anyone else did.

ふたたび、火の鳥が町をおそいました。
火の雨はすべてを焼きはらいます。
「チックタック、もうむりだ！　地下に逃げろ！」
両うでをつかまれ、
チックタックが地下に引きずられていきます。
「はなせ。まだ、あの火のなかにニーナがいるんだ！！」

Now the Fire Bird attacked once more.
Fire consumed everything in the town.
"Mr. Tick-Tock, we have to give up! Quick, escape underground!"
They grabbed Mr. Tick-Tock by both arms,
 and dragged him down with them.
"Let me go! Nina is still in that fire!"

火の雨がやみ、そとに出てみると、
町の景色は変わりはてていました。
それから三日三晩、ニーナをさがしましたが、
ついにみつかりませんでした。
チックタックは時計台にとじこもり、
だれの声にも耳をかさず、
ニーナの葬儀にも参列しませんでした。
「ニーナは死んでいない」

When the rain of fire finally stopped and they all came out again,
they found the town completely changed.
For three days and three nights they searched for Nina,
but they couldn't find her.
Mr. Tick-Tock locked himself away in his clock tower.
He wouldn't listen to what anyone said,
and he didn't go to Nina's funeral.
"Nina isn't dead!" he insisted.

時計台からは、チックタックの泣きごえが、
なんにちもなんにちも
きこえてきました。
すうじつ後、
黒こげになった町のひろばに
ヤクの木が生えているのがみつかりました。
それでも、チックタックはニーナの死を受けいれず、
ただただ時計台のなかで泣きつづけたのです。

Day after day, you could hear Mr. Tick-Tock crying
in the clock tower.
Some days later, in the burnt town plaza,
a Flame Tree was discovered growing.
Even now, Mr. Tick-Tock wouldn't believe that Nina was dead.
He just stayed inside his clock tower, and cried and cried.

ゴロゴロゴロゴロ。
容赦なく時間をきざむ歯ぐるまの音が、時計台にひびきます。
そして時計の針が、チックタックとニーナが約束した
〝１ヶ月後のよるの12時〟をさそうとした、そのときでした。

Rumble rumble rumble rumble!
It was the sound of the cogwheels mercilessly
turning in the clock tower's clock.
Then the time came when the clock's hands were about to reach
that midnight hour one month later,
when Nina and Mr. Tick-Tock had promised to meet.
And that's when it happened…

時計台のすべての歯ぐるまが止まったのです。
チックタックはあわてて確認しましたが、故障はどこにもみあたりません。
時計台は故障したわけではありませんでした。
だれかが止めたわけでもありませんでした。
時計台がじぶんの意思で針を止めたのです。
〝約束の時間〟をさすことを拒否したのです。

All the cogwheels in the clock suddenly stopped.
Mr. Tick-Tock hurried to check everything,
but he couldn't find any problem.
Nothing was broken.
No one had stopped the clock.
It had stopped of its own free will.
It refused to point to "the promised hour."

それからなん年も。
時計台の針は12時をさすことをこばみ、
11時59分で止まったまんま。
だれが修理にきても、時計の針は動きません。
時計台がじぶんの意思で針を止め、
待ちあわせの時間をきざまないことで、
12時の鐘を鳴らさないことで、
チックタックののぞみをつないでいるのです。

Many years passed.
The clock tower's two clock hands were still stuck at 11:59
and refused to move to 12.
It didn't matter who tried to fix it, those hands never moved.
The clock had simply decided not to point to midnight.
It was respecting Mr. Tick-Tock's wishes,
and not ringing the midnight chime that he had promised
to hear with Nina.

「……なるほど。止まったのではなくて、
約束の12時を待っているんですね。
ありがとうございます。話がきけてよかったです」
「そういうことじゃ、修理工。
おまえの出る幕じゃないわい。とっとと役場にかえれ」
「役場にはかえりません。わたしは役場のものではないので」

"I see. So it's not just stopped, it's waiting. Thank you,
I'm glad to have heard the story," said the repairman,
when Mr. Tick-Tock had told him everything.
"That's right. So there's nothing you can do here.
Go off back to the town hall."
"I'm not going back to the town hall. That's not where
I've come from."

「ウソをついてすみません。わたしは役場のものでも、
時計の修理にきたものでもありません」
「だれじゃ？」
「医者です。ニーナさんの主治医をしていました。ニーナさんは、
火の雨がふったあのよるに、死んでなんかいません」
「じょうだんはよせ」
「あのあとも、ニーナさんは、あの呪いと、
けんめいにたたかいつづけたそうです」

"I'm sorry I lied to you. I'm not from the town hall,
 and I didn't come to repair the clock."
"So who are you?"
"I'm a doctor. I was Nina's doctor.
 She didn't really die that night of the rain of fire."
"Is this some kind of joke?"
"After that Nina continued to fight hard against the curse
 she was under."

チックタックが、医師につめよります。
「ニーナは、あのあとも生きていたのか？　だったらなぜ、これまで会いにきてくれなかったんじゃ！！」
「身を引いたんです。ニーナさんも、
あなたに会いたがっていました。
でも、会うわけにはいかなかったのです」
「なんで……」
「ニーナさんが孤児院で世話をしていたカブトムシのからだから、
ヤクの木が生えてきたからです」

When he heard that, Mr. Tick-Tock went to stand
in front of the doctor.
"You mean Nina was still alive after all?
So why didn't she ever come to see me?"
"She stayed away on purpose.
She really wanted to see you, but she couldn't."
"Why?"
"Because a Flame Tree had started growing out of her pet
rhinoceros beetle in the orphanage too."

「ということは、焼けあとからみつかった、
あのヤクの木は……」
「ニーナさんが世話をしていたカブトムシのものでしょう。
彼女を苦しめた呪いの病は遺伝ではなく、
伝染病だったのです」

"So that Flame Tree that started growing from the ruins
 after the fire…"
"That would have been from the rhinoceros beetle.
That curse she suffered from wasn't hereditary.
It was a contagious disease."

「ニーナさんは呪いの病をあなたにうつすわけにはいかなかった。
しかし、ふたりでいると、いつか、
うつしてしまうことになります。
火の雨がふったよる、ニーナさんはみなさんのまえから姿を消し、
呪いの病をひとりで背負う人生をえらんだのです。
わたしが医者の役目を終えるその日まで、彼女は病魔と
たたかいつづけました。
そのあいだもずっと、あなたのことをおもいつづけていました」

"Nina couldn't let you catch her disease, you see.
But if she was with you, that was sure to happen sooner or later.
That night of the rain of fire,
Nina decided to hide herself away from everyone,
and chose to live alone with the burden of her cursed disease.
She went on battling that disease until the day
I was no longer her doctor.
But all that time, she kept on thinking of you!"

もうわたしの出番がなくなったということです。
まだからだの木は残っていますが、根は絶やしたので、
じきになくなるでしょう。呪いの病は、もう完治しています」
そのとき、時計台の階段がきしむ音がきこえました。

"I so wanted to see her!"
"You can tell her that yourself."
"But Nina is…"
"Dead? No, I never said that."
"You just said you stopped being her doctor."
"That was because a vaccine has been invented,
so there is nothing more for me to do. The Flame Tree is still there,
but the root is dead, so the tree will soon disappear.
Her cursed illness is healed."
That was when they heard a creaking sound
from the stairs leading up to the clock.

「待ってくれていたんですね」
ふりかえると、
からだから木を生やした老婆が立っていました。

"You've been waiting for me!"
When Mr. Tick-Tock turned, he saw an old woman standing there, with a tree growing out of her body.

「ごめんなさい。チックタック、
まさか待ってくれているなんておもわなかった。
わたしが死んだことにすれば、あなたが楽になるとおもった。
わたしが死んだことにすれば、あなたのこころは、
つぎの人に向くとおもった」
「バカなことをいうな！　そんなわけないじゃないか！
キミの死を受けいれられるわけないじゃないか！」
「ごめんなさい！　ごめんなさい！　わたしは……
わたしはなん年も、あなたをふりまわしてしまった……」
ニーナは泣きくずれました。

"I'm sorry, Mr. Tick-Tock! I never thought you'd be waiting for me all that time. I thought things would be easier for you if I was dead. I thought you could start to love someone else if you believed I was dead."
"Don't be crazy! How could that ever be true?
And how could I ever accept your death?"
"I'm sorry! I'm so sorry! I...
I put you through that for all these years!"
Nina burst into tears.

ゴロゴロゴロゴロ。
時計台の歯ぐるまがいっせいにまわりだしました。
修理がすんだわけではありません。
だれかがまわしているわけでもありません。
時計台がじぶんの意思で動きだしたのです。
「鳴りますね、12時の鐘が。では、わたしはここで」
そういうと、医師は時計台から出ていきました。

Rumble rumble rumble rumble.
All the cogwheels in the clock tower suddenly began to turn.
They hadn't been repaired.
Nobody was turning them.
The clock was turning of its own free will.
"It's going to chime! The bells for midnight are going to chime. Right, I'll be off."
And the doctor left the clock tower.

「ふたりできくと、約束しただろ？」
「ごめんね、チックタック。待った？」
「ニーナはいつも待ちあわせ時間ギリギリにくるなあ」
「アウト？」
チックタックはくびを横にふり、笑顔でこたえました。

"We promised we'd hear it together, didn't we?"
"Sorry, Mr. Tick-Tock! Did I keep you waiting?"
"You always come just in the nick of time, don't you, Nina?"
"So, I'm late?"
Mr. Tick-Tock shook his head and smiled.

「ギリギリセーフ」

"No, you just made it."

そのよる、
時計台は約束の12時をむかえました。

That night,
the promised hour of 12 o'clock at the clock tower finally arrived.

スタッフ　Credits

絵・文・監督/Illustrator, Writer, Director
西野亮廣　Akihiro Nishino

制作統括/Production Manager（MUGENUP）
アートディレクション/Art Director（MUGENUP）
合成/Compositor（MUGENUP）
アントワーヌ ペラン　Antoine Perrin

絵コンテ/Storyboard Artist
ミズノ シンヤ　Shinya Mizuno

キャラクターデザイン/Character Designers
にしのあきひろ　Akihiro Nishino
ティボー ルクレール　Thibault Leclercq
ピエール クロコ　Pierre Croco

背景デザイン/Background Designers
クラウス ピヨン　Klaus Pillon
ヨナス デ ロ　Jonas De Ro
ミズノ シンヤ　Shinya Mizuno

3Dモデリング/3D Modeler
林 竜太　Ryuta Hayashi

キャラクター制作/Character Artists
ピエール クロコ　Pierre Croco
にしのあきひろ　Akihiro Nishino

背景制作/Background Artists
トム ガーデン　Tom Garden
ピオトル ドゥラ　Piotr Dura
クラウス ピヨン　Klaus Pillon

翻訳/Translator
メレディス マッキニー　Meredith McKinney

翻訳エージェンシー/Translation Agency
近谷浩二（トランネット）　Koji Chikatani (TranNet)

欧文組版アドバイザー/English Typesetting Consultant
コン トヨコ　Rose Toyoko Kon

ブックデザイン/Book Designer
名久井直子　Naoko Nakui

DTP/DTP Operator
小山宏之（美創）　Hiroyuki Koyama (Bisoh)

編集/Book Editors
舘野晴彦（幻冬舎）　Haruhiko Tateno (Gentosha)
袖山満一子（幻冬舎）　Maiko Sodeyama (Gentosha)

出版管理・校正/Printing Manager, Proofreader
田中淳史（幻冬舎）　Atsushi Tanaka (Gentosha)
江幡祥子（幻冬舎）　Shoko Ebata (Gentosha)

マネージメント/Managers
上田浩平（よしもとクリエイティブ・エージェンシー）
Kohei Ueda (Yoshimoto Creative Agency)
須藤啓志（よしもとクリエイティブ・エージェンシー）
Keishi Sudo (Yoshimoto Creative Agency)
松野浩之（よしもとクリエイティブ・エージェンシー）
Hiroyuki Matsuno (Yoshimoto Creative Agency)
鮎川雅江（よしもとクリエイティブ・エージェンシー）
Masae Ayukawa (Yoshimoto Creative Agency)

Special Thanks to
西野亮廣エンタメ研究所　Entertainment Laboratory Akihiro Nishino
満願寺　Manganji-Temple
若田等慧（満願寺）　Toue Wakata (Mangan-ji Temple)
田村有樹子（株式会社にしのあきひろ）　Yukiko Tamura (Akihiro Nishino Co., Ltd.)

〈著者プロフィール〉

にしのあきひろ（西野亮廣）

1980年生まれ。芸人・絵本作家。
モノクロのペン1本で描いた絵本に『Dr.インクの星空キネマ』『ジップ＆キャンディ ロボットたちのクリスマス』『オルゴールワールド』。完全分業制によるオールカラーの絵本に『えんとつ町のプペル』『ほんやのポンチョ』。小説に『グッド・コマーシャル』。ビジネス書に『魔法のコンパス』『革命のファンファーレ』『新世界』。共著として『バカとつき合うな』。有料会員制コミュニティー（オンラインサロン）「西野亮廣エンタメ研究所」は、会員数が2万2000人を突破し、国内最大となっている。

チックタック ～約束の時計台～

2019年4月18日　第1刷発行
2021年1月25日　第7刷発行

著　者　にしのあきひろ

発行者　見城 徹

発行所　株式会社 幻冬舎
　　　　〒151-0051 東京都渋谷区千駄ヶ谷4-9-7
　　　　電話　03(5411)6211(編集)
　　　　　　　03(5411)6222(営業)
　　　　振替　00120-8-767643

印刷・製本所　図書印刷株式会社

検印廃止

万一、落丁乱丁のある場合は送料小社負担でお取替致します。小社宛にお送り下さい。
本書の一部あるいは全部を無断で複写複製することは、法律で認められた場合を除き、著作権の侵害となります。定価はカバーに表示してあります。

©AKIHIRO NISHINO, GENTOSHA 2019
Printed in Japan
ISBN 978-4-344-03448-8　C0095
幻冬舎ホームページアドレス　https://www.gentosha.co.jp/

この本に関するご意見・ご感想をメールでお寄せいただく場合は、
comment@gentosha.co.jp まで。